Her Silent Heart and the Open Sky

a Delta Force romance story
by
M. L. Buchman

Buchman Bookworks

Other works by M.L. Buchman

Newsletter signup at:
www.mlbuchman.com

1

Lashkar Gah, the capital of Helmand Province, Afghanistan—was called the Capital of Hell during the War in Afghanistan. It was hard to believe he was back.

Delta Force operator Sergeant Chris "Deuce" Cooper surveyed the hovel that was their new home. Close by Bost Airport, the only thing it had going for it was it actually had a roof and all four walls. None of the other nearby structures could brag as much.

The insides didn't disappoint; they were equally meager. The walls were adobe, the roof stick, straw, and daubed mud. There wasn't enough rain here to wash it away, especially not in summer. A hundred-plus in the shade and no measurable rain for seven months.

Two small rooms were connected by an archway. It was surprisingly tidy, the hard-packed dirt floor had no buildup of sand from the notorious dust storms. In the front room a battered table, two benches, and three chairs with the backs broken off were neatly arranged. The second room—empty but clean and where they'd be sleeping—showed fresh sweeping marks and not a camel spider or scorpion in sight despite the cool shade.

The other five members of his team surged in out of the midday heat and began dumping heavy packs and bedrolls in the open room.

No one else paid any attention to the cleaning woman. She squatted in a small nook that had a smoky fireplace for burning cow dung and a spot only wide enough for the woman to squat while cooking or lie down and sleep, but not both. She clutched the bundle of bound twigs that was her broom like it was a lifeline—her knuckles white.

She barely looked up as they entered. At his greeting, she'd looked down once more.

Abashed to be an Afghan woman alone with six American soldiers? Or too unintelligent to care? Perhaps a third option.

Command had told them they'd have local help which was a bonus. It meant they wouldn't be living on MREs. She'd know how to shop and cook local chow and he was fine with that. Maxwell and Jaffe, fresh out of training, were new to the squad and it would take them some time squatting over the shitter to build up the right gut flora, but he and the other three operators had walked these roads before and were happy enough to eat local as long as it took no effort on their part.

For himself, a boy raised on pasta and beef in upstate New York, he looked forward to the Afghan cuisine. On previous tours he'd grown a taste for the clean, simple flavors of fresh-baked naan seed bread, rice with tomatoes or lamb and raisins, and Qorma stew. He hoped she was a good cook.

They'd been offered a bunkhouse at Camp Bastion-Leatherneck (now Camp Shorabak), but preferred to be outside anyone else's perimeter—especially the Afghan Armed Forces. They'd been labeled as advisors, but the form of "advice" they were bringing didn't include being in contact with the local forces.

He could see the others assess and forget the servant. Within days they'd think nothing of undressing and crawling into the sack while she puttered about. If she was offended, it would be up to her to leave the room.

"Nothing but wallpaper, man."

Except she wasn't.

Chris noticed that her head scarf was decorative and of the highest quality, or had once been. It was worn thin and time-faded, but it wasn't the scarf of the poorest classes. Its unusual shade of summer green still shone through. Her one vanity left from a former existence? Or stolen from an abandoned home, thoughtlessly left behind years ago by someone with enough money to flee? She posed a lot of questions for him if not for the others.

He didn't make a deal of it, but assigned himself first guard detail and kept an eye out.

She revealed herself in stages as the others sorted gear, shot the shit, and settled in after the long flight. They'd come in on the biweekly commercial flight in ones and twos dressed as

Arab businessmen. They'd grabbed boxes from the cargo that hadn't looked related—their weapons had been in his box labeled as tractor parts. Conway's box was restaurant supply, a month of MREs that they could now not eat. Baxter and Burton smuggled in the comm and surveillance gear and Maxwell and Jaffe, being the new guys, were mainly loaded down with heavy rounds of ammunition and explosives.

As the guys settled, Chris noticed the woman didn't leave the room at random. Rather she found additional tasks until some story was complete: a story told in a language that she had pretended was gibberish to her.

And when she did move, it wasn't with the slow, painful moves of the crone that most of her attire suggested. Nor was it that of a teen. Their servant was a woman who understood English and was intent on keeping that knowledge to herself.

It took a full day before he managed to see her face as she consistently looked down and kept her scarf forward. Every now and then he'd catch her watching them, but she always looked away the moment he turned to face her. Unable to get a good view of her face,

Chris settled on subterfuge, walking close by her and dropping a spoon.

He squatted directly in front of her as she reached for it. Her face—damn but this woman had a face. Clear skin brushed golden-brown, prominent cheekbones, and strong eyebrows that only emphasized the clear dark eyes. The hand that returned the spoon was dirty, but strong and unlined.

He almost said, "Thank you" in Pashto, but at the last moment he switched from "*Ddera manena*" to the Dari "*Tashakor,*" Something about the strength of her face perhaps, or the fullness of her tightly closed mouth.

"*Qabele tashakor nest.*" She looked shocked by her own "You're welcome." She too had spoken in Dari rather than offering the more likely "*Har kela*" in Pashto. Her voice was warm and smooth, with just a little roughness as if she used it only rarely.

In an eyeblink she was gone, not just from the room, but from the house.

Her response meant Dari was probably her native tongue. That would place her home in northern Afghanistan, if she was even Afghani. How had the poor woman ended up in the desert of the far south as a servant? There was no worse place that the country had to offer than Helmand Province. He knew. He'd fought in most of them.

2

Azadah stood by the well, but had brought no water container.

She could go to the market, but it was a long walk and she had just gone this morning to prepare for the American's arrival. It wouldn't matter; the stalls would now be closed in the heat of midday. She had paid a bribe to get the position—a bribe that was only shocking in how meager it had needed to be. How far she had fallen, nothing left but her clothing and her pride.

She stared out at the empty airport. It shimmered in the dry heat. The place where so many planes used to land that there was never silence in Lashkar Gah was now filled only with the wind and the one lone passenger plane that would be leaving soon. That plane was the only safe way to cross back to Kandahar or Kabul—if one had the money. The roads were filled with Afghan checkpoints, Taliban ambushes, and shifting sands.

The American Air Force had staged here and supplied the Marine Corps troops stationed at the great camp north of the city. The British too had been here. They had tried to bring peace. Instead they had given the Taliban a focus and Lashkar Gah had been shredded time after time between the two forces. Now the Taliban came and the Afghan Armed Forces fought them off, but there was little enthusiasm on either side.

But the Americans were back.

There were so few of them, what could they think to accomplish here?

And by asking the question, she knew.

Azadah tipped her head back to look at the skies wondering if she could see it. She couldn't, but didn't doubt that it was there. A drone, impossibly small and far away, circled somewhere above them. Was it looking down at her right now?

"They're very hard to spot," a voice said close behind her.

She looked back down from the sky and was momentarily dizzy. The one they called "Deuce," the one who had tricked her into speaking, had put on a *shalwar kameez*. In the linen drawers and long body shirt, he looked almost native. His beard was short and neat, his hair dark. Only the light brown of his eyes seemed out of place. They were as light as the desert at dusk.

"But they can see us?" Only after she spoke did she realize that again he had tricked her. He had spoken in English and she had replied in the same language.

She had not been caught in years. The last time had earned her a crashing hard slap across the face from an Afghan guard and three months in a prison cell while they debated whether or not to shoot her for spying. The Americans had freed her only when they were recalled back to their country and she could no longer be a threat to them. For a time she feared they would forget about her at the last minute, or perhaps remember. In the end it was as if the three months of her life became nothing.

Azadah prepared to run toward the market, not that she had much hope of losing herself there. Even the watching eye above them would not be needed. She had seen that the man was fleet of foot and he was most certainly armed. This one would have at least three weapons with him: ankle, hip, and at the center of his belly where he could draw it so fast that all she could see was a blur when he did so. He did not have his rifle with him for all of the good it would do her.

But he did not reach for her.

He did not slip a hand into his clothing to hold a weapon.

He did not appear smug about uncovering her secret.

Instead he stood quietly and watched her, waiting until she spoke again.

"What is Deuce? I do not know this word."

"Deuce? It is a playing card for a game with two markers on it. My initials are C. C., Chris Cooper, and they called me that at first. Then 'Two C.' On my third mission, the situation got a little ugly. I solved it by killing two people with one bullet. Luck as much as anything. 'Two C.' became 'Deuce' and it stuck."

His casual tone reassured her as much as anything. "I don't think luck has much to do with your life."

His shrug said maybe. "I met you."

"I work here."

"You are also at the wrong end of your country and speak excellent English."

Not knowing what else to say, Azadah repeated herself, "I work here." These were more words than she had spoken in any language in a year and it was exhausting.

"Who do you work for is the next question."

Security.

It is always security.

Her country no longer spoke of the seasons or the crops. There was less concern for the next dust storm or the birth of a child than of who was aligned with who. There was only, always, security. She was sick of it.

"I speak to no one."

"You're speaking to me. I guess that makes me no one," he managed to sound hurt.

And she almost smiled, but she was too out

of practice. "Yes, it is as I said. I speak to *no one*. I work here."

"Cleaning?"

"Yes."

"And cooking?"

"Yes, and carrying water."

"Which you must carry in your cupped palms," he pointed at her empty hands.

"And I watch men itch and scratch while they have nothing to do," she shot back at him, piqued at being caught. She did not like that he knew exactly how much he had surprised her.

"I'm talking to you. That counts as doing something."

Azadah stared at him for a long moment. This man they called Two C.—she did not like the way "Deuce" felt on her tongue—*was* talking to her. He was not interrogating her. He had not struck her or arrested her. He was *talking* to her. He already knew more about her than she had revealed to anyone in a long time.

Did he somehow also know that her parents had fled Iran during the fall of the Shah and their great mistake had been fleeing to the east? They had arrived in Afghanistan at the same time as the Russians. She'd been born in the midst of "Russia's Vietnam," a fifteen-year disaster for both countries in which a million Afghan civilians were killed and six million fled their homeland entirely.

Rushing to the relative safety of the Mujahideen, they had served as skilled administrators. The American-backed rebels' success against the Russians had come to nothing when the tribes then fell to fighting among themselves.

Then Mohammed Omar had taken those hard-learned fighting skills and left-over American weaponry and formed the Taliban. Another half-million Afghans had died, including her parents, before Osama bin Laden's bombing of New York had forced the Americans to face what they had helped create.

In each incarnation, Azadah's lot had slipped lower and lower. She'd been born to senior government officials. She'd grown up in the administration centers of a nationwide insurgency. She had cowered during the rule of the Taliban as a clerk; invaluable because she knew everyone and every connection, reviled because of her sex.

And now she had become a cleaner and cook for this man.

He was not a big man, no more than any Afghan. She was tall for a woman and only had to look upward a hand's width when speaking with him.

"Why are you here, Two C.? Why have you Americans come back?"

His smile acknowledged her preference for his older nickname. He pointed to the scant shade afforded by the side of a house. There was no roof and through the windows there was only rubble—a casualty of the 2008 Taliban bombardment of the city. She couldn't remember the family who'd lived there and that bothered her. It was as if she'd just become disconnected from her own country.

She followed him there out of the sun. She'd forgotten how much the Americans hated the heat and the brightness. He did not stand too close. It wouldn't be right. If she were anybody, she might be shunned by the community for even speaking with a lone male—and if the Taliban were in control she might be beaten or even killed—but she wasn't and for the moment they weren't, so perhaps it didn't matter.

"We are here," he told her once they were settled, "because the Taliban see the weaknesses in the Afghan Armed Forces as opportunity. We have learned that great force is not the answer here. It was me and people like me who cut the head off the snake. We have come to do it again."

Azadah leaned back against the wall suddenly tired of it all. She had fought so long, her family had given so much, and once more they had come full circle.

This man from a land so foreign she could scarcely imagine it had left his home and come back to Afghanistan.

"The head of this snake will always grow anew." Perhaps he heard the resignation in her voice, the hopeless battle that was Afghanistan. Her country had once been rich in art and literature, if not money. Now, after forty years of war, the country barely had buildings.

"Then," Two C. said with a calm confidence that forced her to look back at his quiet face. "We will come back and cut it off again."

3

Chris knew not to trust a pretty face—no matter how goddamn striking—he hadn't joined the service just yesterday.

But he considered himself a better than average judge of human character, and there were things about his woman that didn't fit together. At least not if she was a spy, infiltrator, or saboteur.

"May I ask your name?"

"Azadah. So true, is it not?" Despite her obvious soul-deep weariness, she was still capable of humor.

Her name: independent, free.

She struck him as a woman trapped…but not subdued. *Qawi* perhaps. The word meant both strong and powerful. But *manda* as well, so weary that she could scarce stand under her own weight.

He'd done many tours in Iraq and Afghanistan. Handled more than a few operations in places better not mentioned beyond the borders of Iran and Pakistan. In some places no Arab woman would think to speak with him.

Yet Azadah spoke with him. And she showed of herself who she was.

"I'm inclined to trust you, Azadah."

"I am trustworthy," she said without looking at him. "Or I was. Now I no longer know. I do what I do."

He too leaned back against the mud wall to look out across the area. This whole section of houses had been abandoned. Storms had piled the dust in odd drifts against the few remaining walls. But, like any poor culture, anything that could be salvaged had been. There was little waste, merely the tan-dusted wreckage of what had once been a community.

The city of Lashkar Gah had grown from

two-hundred thousand to two-fifty over the last decade, but still that had not been enough to push people back into this ravaged corner of the older city. Dating back a thousand years, the city's ill-fated name translated as "Army Barracks" and described only too well its war-torn history.

The brush of a breeze invaded their bit of stolen shade with a slap of heat that experience told him he would never fully adapt to in their time here.

"The place I come from is a land of water and trees," he didn't know quite why he was telling her this. "It is called the Finger Lakes and is in the far west of our New York State. The lakes are long, thin, and spread like a hand. The country is so beautiful that the local tribes said it was where God rested his hand after finishing creation." He could almost see it, laid like a green mirage over the desolate land before him.

She did not answer for a very long time. When she did, her words were almost a soft caress.

"Thank you. I can almost see your land of green. It is good to believe such places exist."

And then, in that way she had, Azadah was gone and he stood alone in the shrinking wedge of shade formed by a broken wall.

4

Three days later Chris found a slip of paper on his pillow. It lay so close to his nose that it should have tickled.

It was an address and a name. A name that had him sitting up sharply and not bothering to wonder how the paper had arrived there without him waking. Abdullah bin Hazar wasn't at the top of their target list, but he wasn't at the bottom either.

Chris snapped his fingers and the rest of the team came awake. Maxwell had been on guard, in between predictable trips to the shitter. Somehow he too had missed the delivery of the slip of paper. Because, Chris knew, no one but him saw Azadah, now a fixture in their midst.

She had been so stealthy that she hadn't disturbed his sleep, which made him uncomfortable. He preferred the idea that she was already a familiar presence in his mind so that his unconscious vigilance had let her come so close. They had not spoken again, but he couldn't help tracking her movements whenever she was in or near the building. She revealed the depth of their mutual awareness when he would glance around unexpectedly and find her watching him. At first, her gaze had flinched away, but just last night she had watched him for a long moment before, he'd swear, she'd blushed and looked down.

Rather than show the slip of paper around as it would cause too many questions, he jumped straight in.

"The third building to the south of the road to Marjeh, close by the Helmand River. Get me everything we know."

The team snapped to. In moments they had the drone retasked and feeding them images. A small compound less than a kilometer away, it would be overlooking the river if not for its high wall.

"I've got three late-model SUVs out front and four armed guards," Conway reported. The "Con Man" had been Chris' right-hand man through some ugly shit and, as usual, was hunched over the drone controls. They couldn't actually fly the thing from here, those guys lived in a hole in Nevada, but they could take over the camera feed and streaming video archive as needed.

Three new SUVs. Not unheard of, but certainly not common in this city.

"I have cell transmissions," Baxter reported.

"Who doesn't these days?" Burton countered.

The two of them were like a Laurel and Hardy routine; never just one spoke. They'd been collectively tagged as "BB" because they would sometimes chatter back and forth like a BB gun plinking away at tin cans.

"CIA at Langley has squat." "Try The Activity." "Duh! Already on it!" The two of them were one of the sharpest electronic surveillance teams in the business.

Chris let the sound of his team working the

problem blend into the background. He was watching the silent woman who lay unmoving on the floor before the hearth. She was curled up with her shawl pulled over her face as she typically did while sleeping. Her hand clutched her shawl tightly as it always did, as if it was her last sliver of hope. But now her breathing was different. He watched the uneven acceleration of the movement of her ribcage.

"The Activity has nothing." "Cell phone transmissions are not in the clear."

Encrypted signals. They were getting smarter about not being overheard. He knew Baxter would route them to Burton to send back for possible decryption.

"Running back the video," Conway was on it. The drone had a camera system that could see the entire width and length of the city. The resolution was so high they could zoom in on a small area like the compound, and then roll time backwards.

"Two SUVs were on the move three hours ago. One traces to another compound on the northeast side of the city, but the second one had arrived from the direction of Kandahar to the east. Close-ups coming in."

Chris moved up to sit on the bunk next to Jaffe who was working the current drone feed rather than the historic one. But he managed to align himself so that a darkened screen reflected the "sleeping" Azadah. Moments after he turned his back, she indeed raised a lazy hand to remove her shawl. *Couldn't resist looking, could you?*

Chris glanced over his shoulder to let her know she'd been caught. Rather than a blush, she met his gaze for three long heartbeats.

She was watching him. Waiting to see what he would do with the information she'd provided. Had she set a trap for them?

For perhaps the first time in his whole military career he was going to consciously choose to engage an unknown area on the advice of an unknown civilian. He only knew her name, her beauty, and her weariness. *If you're an agent, you're damn good at your job, lady.*

She made no reply to his unspoken thought, instead turned away to tend the low fire.

In half an hour they had the compound clearly in their heads and a plan of action. His core team knew the faces of all of the main players on their target, but he made sure they reviewed Abdullah bin Hazar's photo again. He assigned the new guys to backup roles until he had a better feel for them.

They'd already acquired several vehicles. Bost Airport was like a junkyard. Cars left behind by departing businessmen. Trucks that were too worn for the evacuating US forces to bother taking or permanently disabling. They'd spent the last few days putting together a small but serviceable fleet of unremarkable appearance.

Once ready, they dispatched out of the building. It would be twilight soon. They'd leave now and do some daytime scouting. Then they'd wait for nightfall and slide in from three directions at once.

Chris let the others go out, then stepped over to the kitchen from which Azadah hadn't reemerged.

She was waiting for him, he could tell even though she still squatted with her back turned.

"Abdullah?" He asked, meaning far more than confirming their target.

She nodded without turning.

"You'll still be here when we get back." He was careful to not make it a question.

Again her nod, then so softly that he could barely hear her, "I have nowhere else to go."

He left her there and followed his men out into the yard.

"Hitting on the maid servant, Deuce?" Conway teased him as Chris slid into the driver's seat of a ten-year old silver Toyota Corolla. It was a small and awkward car to launch an attack from if they were surprised, but over half of the cars on the road were aged Corollas, so it was as good as invisible.

"Looking to be put into an early grave, Conway?" Azadah wasn't the sort of woman who a man just yanked down her *partug* and took from behind. One look in her eyes told him that. Easy women existed. Even in a conservative place like this country, there were plenty of willings, both unpaid and paid. Azadah was not one of them.

"Well, now that you—"

"Just drive!"

5

Azadah stared into the small fire and wondered at the enormity of what she'd done. The two cars and a truck had departed and the echoing silence of the evening settled over the house.

For three days the six men had been constantly here, at least some of them. She'd never been alone except during the short walk to the well or the long walk to market. Often they went out in ones or twos on lazy "patrols," ambling along just like any local. But she'd heard the reports when they returned and how they were familiarizing themselves with an impressive amount of detail about the city. Two hundred thousand people in an area roughly three by five kilometers, yet they soon knew it as well as many who had spent their lives here.

Now, there was only her own breathing, the bleating of a distant goat, and the silence that was Afghanistan.

She…liked Two C. She liked her own joke of calling him that, partly because the man Chris was overwhelming. She'd seen how the others followed him, always wanting his good opinion, asking his advice. These warriors, America's very best, respected him deeply and listened carefully when he spoke.

It was rare for him to speak first which she also liked about him. He too understood the value of listening.

That was how she'd heard about Abdullah. A chance comment in the market had led her to walk far across the city and listen as she followed a goat that wasn't hers by the compound's gates in the great stone wall.

She knew this once had been an American city, even called "Little America" by some. They had come during the Cold War and built dams and waterways to create a massive irrigation system across the surrounding desert. They had built roads, homes, swimming pools...all of which had ultimately failed. Some farming occurred here, but the great agricultural plenty promised in the 1950s and 60s had been gone long before the Russians invaded in the late 1970s. Instead, the open-plan American style of buildings had been closed in after they left with three-meter high walls.

One of these had been taken over by Taliban leader Abdullah bin Hazar.

But why had she told the Delta Force soldier?

Why had she exposed herself to hope once more?

It was a question she had not answered when the twilight fell, nor when the men returned just hours before the dawn.

She listened to the footsteps. There was an excitement. There was an energy in the air that she'd forgotten the feeling of. There was a slap of weary bodies collapsing onto thick bedrolls as the soldiers dropped down on them. Weapons rattled.

One set of footsteps crossed to the threshold

that separated the sleeping and the kitchen area. They stopped there, unmoving.

Azadah reached out to nurse the fire back to life and to begin the cooking of breakfast.

The meal was nearly ready before she heard the footsteps move away.

6

"I want Syed!" Jaffe growled as he slammed down his gear.

It wasn't even worth responding. They all wanted him, Chris most of all. Their three-month tour was up in just a few more days and the Taliban leader for all of Helmand had eluded them so far.

He had been there. Even during the first operation when they'd taken down Abdullah and a local lieutenant. While they'd been scouting the compound, one of the three Range Rovers had departed. Not knowing who was in it, they had let it go. When Chris finally gave the team the go, Abdullah had died in the first round. But before his lieutenant bled out he reported that Syed Harim Akhram had indeed been there earlier and just left.

Three months they had been chasing him back and forth across the countryside, twice over the ninety miles to Kandahar but with no success.

After their initial success with Abdullah, command had taken a real interest in their operation. A heavier drone had been lofted with more sophisticated communications detection and an even better camera. Computing assets had been layered in behind that to intercept and interpret cell and radio communications in real time.

For three months they had become a jacked-up, head-of-snake-eradicating machine. Three of the senior-level people, along with dozens of minor ones, had been tracked and taken down due to the millions of dollars of effort.

Yet five other top Taliban leaders had been taken down by tiny slips of paper left on his pillow while he slept through the heat of the day. He didn't know Azadah's wages, but assumed it was typical for the region, a hundred Afghanis. A dollar and a half a day.

Also for three months, they had barely spoken again. Only when the day was done and the first stars shone across the desert sky, sometimes she would come and sit by him. He'd imagine they were looking over a different landscape, one of rolling green hills, grazing cows, and cool forest. He would grill lamb and chicken Spiedie kebabs and would serve them to her in a fold of sesame-seed crusted Italian scali bread as the sky faded and the stars ruled the summer sky.

More than once he fell asleep with his back propped against the wall and his feet crossed together on the sand, listening to her silence. But he always woke alone, never hearing her leave.

7

Three days!

Azadah had never felt so helpless. They would be gone in three days and she would be…lost. How was one woman's heart supposed to hold so many emotions?

She shouldn't care!

Others had come and gone. So why did these men tear at her so?

They had been thoughtlessly kind to her and she would miss them. They had eaten heartily of the food she'd made them and occasionally even thought to thank her.

Five of them had treated her so.

But the sixth—

Unable to stand the thought, she snatched her market basket and fled from the house.

They had done exactly as Two C. had promised; they had cut the head off the snake, or at least most of it. She had seen no prisoners, heard of none. Maybe the Americans had finally learned that a dead terrorist was far simpler than a live one.

She knew Syed plagued them and twice she'd heard almost enough to find him, but not quite. Not without exposing herself more than she dared.

No one knew about "her men" as she'd come to think of them. People certainly knew what they were doing though. She could see the effect in the way the Afghan Armed Forces had increased their patrols through the city. As she made her way into the market she could see that they held their heads a little higher. People even waved at them on occasion as if it was their doing. The heavy mantle that was the Taliban was once again lifting its smothering weight from the city. Maybe this time it would even be enough.

But her men were leaving.

Worse, her *man* was leaving.

In her panic, her feet had carried her to the edge of the market, for where else had she to go. She slowed and joined the others in the lazy heat, but her mind would not settle.

How would a day be without Chris "Two C." Cooper to smile at her when he was pleased? How could she possibly wake up and not see him there, sleeping so close by her that she felt like she existed, like she mattered once more? And perhaps worst of all, to never again sit beside him as evening fell and feel the peace inside the man, no matter his duty of death?

She had been invisible for so long that it should be easy to go back to her old habits. But not this time. He saw her in a way no one ever had before. And she saw him so clearly. His effortless leadership. His simple rough brand of kindness that made his men both respect and trust him.

How could she—

And then she heard it.

An old serving woman who she recognized as Abdullah bin Hazar's cook, the woman who had unwittingly led her to that first discovery. She was complaining of the load she must carry and the food she must cook. It was a common complaint heard about the market, especially when a feast was planned. But who was she cooking for now? There was no holy feast day coming.

Once a trusted servant of the Taliban, always one?

Perhaps. Just perhaps.

She did what she could to keep within listening range. She studied the pretty dye powders while the woman bought cauliflower and onion. She inspected the scrawny chickens on offering while the woman bought a lamb and drank tea while it was slaughtered and the meat was dressed.

Azadah did not have to stay too close as the woman's complaints were not soft.

"With no warning. Big guest coming to town. Many people."

Azadah wanted to follow, but how to do so discreetly?

"Very important man. Very important guests."

And that was when Azadah made her mistake. She stood in one place watching for too long and the old woman turned on her.

"You. You are the quiet one who speaks to no one. I've heard about you."

It wasn't a question and all Azadah could think to do was nod.

"And no man."

"What makes you say that, mother?" She forced out the words, and it seemed the respectful thing to say.

"Your basket is empty yet."

"Yours is very full." So much so that the woman was badly burdened with it. And then Azadah had an idea. "May I help with yours? Do you have far to go?"

"A sweet girl. But I can only pay a little," the woman eyed her shrewdly.

Azadah knew her clothes were tattered and worn. She had not even dusted them off after rising from the hearth before she rushed out the door.

"Even a pittance would help," she tipped her empty basket as an explanation only then realizing that in her haste she had left all of her money tucked under the third rock from the left of the fireplace. Her pockets were as empty as her basket.

"Let's see how you fare."

And so simply, Azadah fell in with Geti and began helping her with the shopping.

8

Chris had seen Azadah run out the door, basket in hand even though she'd already been to the market once this morning. He was now so familiar with her ways that he knew something was deeply wrong, but he'd been ill prepared to follow. His sidearms were spread in pieces before him for cleaning and he was not properly clothed to blend into the city.

By the time guns were assembled and he was dressed, he knew there was no point in attempting to follow. Besides, he and Conway were the only two at the house. He'd sent the other two teams out to scour the streets. Over the last three months they had each built up a circle of friendly contacts and now was the time to tap them—one last shot at Syed.

Conway was on guard.

"Which way did she go?"

"She who?" Conway looked truly perplexed. He scanned out the window, then turned to inspect the rooms. "Oh. Servant girl? No idea. Thataway," he waved a hand toward the city.

Chris stood on the threshold squinting against the burning sun. He couldn't wait to get back to a land where people wore sunglasses. Afghanis never seemed to squint or be bothered by the brightness of the day, and since they were undercover they couldn't either.

Ten minutes. She'd had a head start of under ten minutes. But today was Thursday. That made tonight the end of the work week and tomorrow a day of prayer. It was the biggest market of the week, stretching blocks. It would be packed and he'd have no chance of finding her in the crowd.

The "wrongness" of her actions was itching at his intuition. After three months he was shocked she even *could* surprise him. Every gesture, every breath, the quiet hum when she was happy about a task, even the way she looked at him when she didn't think he was watching.

Yet something had grabbed her by the throat. If she were a more effusive woman, he'd have expected an outright scream based on the way she'd fled.

Again he went to step across the threshold, but again he stopped.

He had no way to follow her.

…unless he did.

Chris spun on his heel and dug under the other gear for one of the equipment briefcases and dropped it on the table.

"What the hell, Deuce?"

He ignored Conway. His training said to let her go. She had proven herself too many times for her to be a threat. Besides, if she were betraying them, she would not have acted so obviously out of character.

But the man in him had only found one way to interpret her actions: panic. And she'd become far too important for him not to protect her, or at least try.

He *did* have a way to follow her.

"C'mon! C'mon! C'mon!" The computer was taking forever to boot up.

9

Azadah's arms were soon burning with the load she'd been given to carry; Geti had seen opportunity and shifted all of the heavy items to Azadah's basket. They moved out beyond the last awning of the market and headed north across the city. No car waited, nor a cart. Though the woman was stout and old, she continued to move steadily along despite her burden.

Not a word had passed between them as they shopped, though Geti had plenty to say to the shopkeepers.

"This is for a very special man. Most very

ery important man. You must give me your best, but at your best price."

Azadah was at first impressed at the prices Geti could get from the merchants, but soon learned to watch their expressions. Some were cautious men, where others looked eager to curry favor. The more she watched, the more she was convinced that she was right. The "important man" must be Syed Harim Akhram, the Taliban commander for all of Helmand Province.

She must get word back to Two C., but she couldn't think of how. Once she'd seen the man Jaffe on the far side of the market. But his glance had slid right by her without recognition and then he was gone.

Beyond the final awning of the market, the cool morning was made hot by the bright sun. She glanced up at the sky, a hazy blue that—

The sky!

Somewhere up there—

She turned her face upward as if warming it in the sun's rays for as long as she dared. She did this again at each turning as they crossed the city.

Now she could only hope.

10

Chris scrolled back ten minutes and then zoomed the recording of the drone's data feed on their little house.

Nothing. Nothing. Nothing. At five minutes he knew he'd missed her. He'd spent too long in indecision.

He rolled backwards faster and faster.

At seventeen minutes back, he found her.

He began scrolling forward at two times speed.

She had rushed out the door. In accelerated mode she practically flew.

He lost her several times with the joystick

because when she turned the corner of the street and was out of sight of the house, she'd run as if the very devil was after her.

Chris finally had to slow down the feed while he was still fourteen minutes behind her because she'd reached the edge of the market. Finally he had to go back to real time and growl in frustration at being stuck fourteen minutes behind her actual actions.

Had it not been for her head scarf, he'd never have been able to track her at all. But the summer green stood out in a sea of blues, grays, and blacks. There were a few scarves that were sunshine yellow and others were ornately decorated, but none like hers.

Besides, now that he was again watching her at normal speed, he'd know it was her anywhere. He'd watched her in the market before when she didn't know he'd spotted her. She walked with her head up and a confidence in her stride that she kept carefully hidden at the house, but was still completely her. All he had to do was watch for a woman who walked like she was the embodiment of summer.

She disappeared beneath an awning and he was momentarily stumped. Then he zoomed back just enough for the edges of the awning to show to all sides of the computer screen.

There!

Crossing the gap between the first stall and the next to the north.

She was moving in no pattern he could detect. It was hard to tell, even at maximum resolution, but her basket appeared to still be empty.

Then she was under one broad awning for so long he was afraid he'd missed her. Just as he was about to scroll back, she stepped once more across a gap. This time she had something in her basket and she was accompanied by another scarf-clad woman. It was the first time he'd ever seen her with another person since—

"Think she's selling us out?"

"Shit!" Chris jumped at finding Conway leaning in over his shoulder to stare at the screen. He'd hit the joystick hard and swung the view several streets to the side. "Damn it, Con Man! No, I don't."

"Jumpy, Deuce. You so hot for the old biddy?"

Chris looked up at him. The man hadn't even looked closely enough to see the beautiful woman hiding in their midst.

Hiding.

What if Conway was right and he was wrong? What if—

"Shut up! Go away!"

Conway shrugged, "Nothing better to do. Jaffe and Maxwell are back. Didn't find shit. So I put them on guard. Better find her again."

Chris kept his snarl to himself. He didn't even know where he'd lost her because he'd been following stall to stall, not going down the street. By the time he located her again, he was over nineteen minutes behind.

He again found where she picked up the companion—older companion by how she moved.

Soon they were both heavily burdened and had exited the market…to the north.

"That's sure not the way back to us," Conway had sat down close beside him.

It wasn't and he was worrying at it when he saw Azadah pause.

She paused…and turned her face to the sky.

It was the moment that had captivated him three long months ago.

But they can see us? She'd asked as she

looked for a drone that a very smart woman had known was above them.

Her face then had been so clear. Lit by the sun, her skin had a luminosity that made a man want to kneel before it. That was the moment he would always count as their first meeting. Not when he'd tricked her into speaking Dari, but when he'd seen her face kissed by the sun.

Even though the camera resolution wasn't high enough, his memory was able to easily paint her expression upon the screen.

Do you see me, Two C.? Look, Two C., I'm right here.

He followed the two women up the street. Now that they'd left the covering of the market, it was easy to regain some of the lost minutes on her.

At the next turn, she looked once more to the sky. She looked directly at the drone, her face square into the camera, even though she couldn't possibly know exactly where it was.

He could almost hear her begging him to follow.

"Call everyone in. This is our shot."

Conway didn't move from his side, but

was now watching him rather than the small computer screen.

"Trust me. Go."

11

"She helped you carry groceries?" The guard hadn't pointed his AK-47 right at her, but it was loose in his hands.

"Yes. A very nice girl. Now pay her fifty Afghanis and she'll be on her way."

The guard reached out a big hand and yanked back the scarf that Azadah had pulled forward as they'd approached.

"Kurdish," he cursed studying her face. "A long way from home, girl." He kept his hand clamped in her hair forcing her to raise her chin. "You spy for Americans or Iranians?"

Geti squinted up at her face and Azadah

could see the suspicion forming in the old woman's eyes. Azadah knew it would be a mistake to protest her innocence, but she couldn't think of what else to do. She had to get away, but there was no way to do so without raising more suspicions. So, she'd make up something else.

"For fifty more Afghanis, I will help you cook, mother," she addressed the woman, though the guard still had her head wrenched back. A hundred was a full day's wages. "For even twenty. My basket was as empty as my belly."

"I think she'd do better waiting with me," the guard shifted his grip to clamping onto her neck in a suggestive way.

"You!" She slapped at his chest. "You unhand this innocent woman. I am for the man who marries me, not someone like you." And when she imagined this man touching her rather than Two C., who had never touched her at all, she couldn't stand it. Acid surged in her belly and she pulled back and spat in the man's face.

His hand struck her so fast that she never saw it coming.

She was sprawled in the dirt and all she

could think through the slashing pain was that the vegetables and meat she had carried were going to spoil in the hot sand.

She tried to gather them up even though she could barely see through the pain and flashes of light.

12

"God damn it!" Chris watched the slap send Azadah flying.

He bolted up off his chair and would have knocked the laptop to the floor if Conway hadn't grabbed it.

Chris yanked out his sidearm and looked around, but there was no one to shoot. She wasn't here. That goddamn bastard guard—who was going to die slowly, painfully, and begging for mercy from a god he'd never see because he'd roast in hell even if Chris had to escort him there personally—wasn't here either.

"Look."

He did. And all he saw were four dirty walls, too much gear, and no Azadah.

"Look," Conway repeated and tapped the screen.

Chris knew he was being a fool. He slammed his sidearm back in its holster and was now looking over Conway's shoulder.

Slowly, painfully, Azadah was gathering up the shopping items that had been spilled out of her basket. There was a lot of food there. The second woman was facing off the guard who was actually the one backing away, and her basket wasn't empty either. Then the older woman began helping Azadah refill her basket, climb to her feet, and then led her through the gate.

The moment before she stepped inside the house, Azadah didn't take one last look at the guard. She took one last look at the sky.

And then was gone from the screen.

13

Azadah wished she had made different choices.

Wished she hadn't paid the bribe to get the job of cooking and cleaning for the Americans. Wished she hadn't helped them. Wished she hadn't befriended Geti in the market. And wished she hadn't spit in the guard's face. Already her left eye was swelling shut as Geti tut-tutted about the kitchen and then smeared on a cool salve against the rising heat.

"Nice to see a girl with character. Not very common anymore. Women bareheaded in public. I don't like it. The western music they play. I like that not at all."

Azadah reached up and felt her own bare head, then slid her hand down to her neck where the brute of a guard had grabbed her. No scarf. Her mother's scarf, the last she had of her family's possessions was gone. It was—

"Here you are," Geti's hands were gentle as she lifted the green scarf and wrapped it carefully about Azadah's head.

Even the lightest touch of cloth had her hissing in pain, but she didn't pull away.

"I could use the help and I don't think Mahmood is going to like it if you try to leave."

Once again she had been trapped. Successive cages had driven her south, except beyond Lashkar Gah there had been nowhere else to go. To the south lay only Dasht-e-Margow, the "Desert of Death."

So Azadah did what she must do; as she had so many times before.

She must survive.

She went to her basket and began sorting through the goods and dusting off the sand.

14

"It's a goddamn fortress," Conway leaned against the hood of their white Corolla. They had driven by it once which let them view three sides and were now parked a kilometer away where field became hard desert and there was no one to overhear them. In the heat of the day there wasn't even anyone to see them.

Baxter and Burton had passed by the back the compound in a small delivery truck and nodded in agreement.

"We only saw the one guard earlier."

"Now there are ten."

"And that's only outside the wall."

"What about air support?"

Chris shook his head. "No one available helicopters. No additional teams either. They've got a big push going against a Taliban training camp and ammunition supply chain up by Khost. All they can offer us is a C-130."

"A Spooky?" Conway sounded excited. A "Spooky" was one of the awe-inspiring gunships in the American arsenal. It could level the compound in minutes with pinpoint accuracy from thousands of feet up, or it could cut a hole in the wall and not touch the building.

"Nope. Cargo. On the ground in Kabul so they need two hours notice to get here."

"So it's just the six of us, one cargo plane, and a pile of bad guys."

"Don't forget the drone." The BB team put in. "Four Hellfires aboard." "Punch an awesome hole." "Delivered and done."

Chris sagged against the hood, and then jolted upright because the metal had become scorching hot under the sun.

"There's a civilian in there."

"Sure, cooks, servants, probably a couple of wives or whores," Conway shrugged. "This is a major goddamn meeting. This is paydirt. We got to take them out."

Chris groaned and scowled at the ground. It's exactly what Washington was pushing him to do. They hadn't spotted Syed yet. Because Chris didn't trust what Washington would tell him, he had Jaffe and Maxwell back at the house watching the camera feed.

No one doubted Syed would come. It looked as if he was coming to anoint the already-gathering next tier of Taliban leadership to replace those his team had spent the last three months removing. There hadn't been a target like this since the Al-Shabaab training camp in Somalia when a hundred and fifty fighters had been taken down in a single raid.

Washington pushing? Hell! They were going to order an airstrike the minute they confirmed Syed's arrival.

"I repeat, there's a civilian in there." Chris pictured Azadah's last pleading look to the sky as if begging him to come find her.

"What? Our maid?" Conway turned on him. "You're fucking worried about a nobody maid when we've got Syed in our sights?" Then he got a look in his eye. "I *knew* the bitch was putting out for you. Stingy bastard, Deuce, not sharin—"

Chris had never struck a fellow soldier before, but he didn't even think. Conway was four inches taller and several inches broader than he was and Chris laid him out in the dirt.

BB grabbed either of his arms, but he wasn't on the attack. This wasn't some battle.

Conway shook his head trying to clear it and then glared up at him from the dirt.

Chris shrugged and Baxter and Burton let him go but stayed close enough to grab him again if needed.

"Go ahead," Conway turned and spat some blood into the dust. "Deny it. You want to blow off a major kill for bit of stuff."

Chris ignored him and looked to the sky. Just as Azadah had, seeking the drone. Seeking an answer. Seeking help.

"That 'bit of stuff'—who I never touched by the way, asshole—gave us Abdullah. She gave us Majeed, Patris, Wais, and Temur. And now she's given us Syed." Then he looked back down at his teammates. "And if we don't have a better plan ready to go on a moment's notice,

Washington is going to pay her back with a one-way ticket to hell."

"She did? The maid was your contact?" Conway stared up at him in shock. "You always had the best leads and none of us ever knew how."

It was more like he was her contact. It was her need to cleanse the land and he had become her instrument of destruction.

"So, we need a plan and we need it fast." He offered a hand to Conway and dragged him up off the dirt. By the strength of their shared handclasp, he knew they were square.

This time it was Conway who looked to the sky, "How long can you hold off Washington?"

"Not very."

"Then," Conway looked down at him and offered the cheerfully evil smile that had made him Chris' right-hand man for so many tours. "How do you feel about car bombs?"

Chris thought about it for a moment, "Do I have to be driving it when it goes off?"

Conway slapped him on the shoulder and they headed back toward their camp.

15

By the time everything was in place, night had fallen. The temperature was down into the breathable eighties and Chris was sweating more than he did standing out in the midday sun. Dry lightning crackled over the city as it so often did—bright flashes, sharp cracks, and no promise of rain.

He sat at the wheel of the Corolla four blocks and one turn from the terrorists' compound and wished there was a different solution.

But then, as he waited, he could feel the operation-mode take over. There was no past

or future within the heart of an operation—
only the moment.

For the third time in the last hour his radio
crackled to life. "White SUV inbound."

The last two had driven by and continued
on into the heart of the city. The compound lay
at the end of Lashkargah 2 Road at the north
edge of the city.

Like most Afghan cities, Lashkar Gah
didn't peter out. There were houses crowded
together, only distinguishable by their
differing styles of protective walls and the
color of the door, and then the city ended.
The compound was an anomaly, almost as
assuredly as bin Laden's massive compound
had been. They'd had twenty SEALs, a half
dozen helos, and no friendlies inside. He had
half a dozen Delta Force operators and—

"Chain of SUVs. Counting five," the drone's
pilot reported. With only the six of them,
Chris had needed every asset on the ground.
He hated depending on some fool with his
butt parked in a Nevada bunker, but didn't
have a choice.

"Arriving at compound. Unloading. Count
twenty-two additional on the ground."

He could practically hear Conway swearing somewhere in the distance. Six Delta and now over forty armed bad guys.

"Syed Harim Akhram confirmed. I repeat. Syed Harim Akhram confirmed."

Past thinking, Chris dropped into gear and put his foot down on the gas.

He heard Conway's radio call of "Friendlies in the compound" that would delay Washington long enough for it to be true. Hopefully. If not, he and the Hellfire missiles should arrive at about the same time.

Four blocks. The engine groaned and the suspension wallowed, but the tough little car began accelerating.

First gear, then he finally nursed the overloaded Corolla into second.

Turning the corner, he had three straight blocks with the compound's gate in full view. Perhaps he'd have another block before the guards heard the straining engine.

Maxwell had cut the power to the local neighborhood at sunset, carefully leaving the compound lit. That way there would be no lights shining on him, but no suspicions raised prematurely.

If he was lucky, maybe they wouldn't see him for two of the three remaining blocks.

He wasn't paying enough attention and hit a pothole. For a second he was afraid he'd broken the frame and their plans would die right here. But it held and the car continued accelerating despite the extra thousand pounds of cargo.

He cursed that cruise controls wouldn't engage until a car was going thirty miles an hour. He was less than half a block from the gates when he hit the thirty-minimum speed.

The first spray of bullets from the gate guard shattered the windshield.

Chris hit the headlights on high-beam and saw the guards raise arms to shield their eyes. It gave him a moment to latch the hook over the steering wheel to hold it on course.

Jaffe had pre-rigged the driver's door so that when Chris pulled the handle, it didn't open—it fell off completely.

One last check…a hundred feet to go… he rolled out of the car and slammed into the ground hard. He spun and slid a dozen yards, almost missing his planned hide.

He dove behind the low wall at the same

moment the plunger detonators on the front of the car hit the main gate.

A thousand pounds of fertilizer taken from agricultural sheds, diesel siphoned from one of the many disabled trucks at the airport, and most of their supply of C-4 exploded.

A blinding sheet of white filled the sky like midday, brighter than a lightning strike, and reflected off the surrounding buildings. The shock wave came next and the low wall collapsed on him.

Too wound up to know if he was hurt, Chris jumped to his feet just as BB crashed their car into two guards who'd somehow survived the initial blast.

Conway drove by in a heavy truck. He slowed just enough for Chris to grab onto the back and be dragged into the bed by Maxwell and Jaffe.

They plowed blindly through the fire that had once been the front gate and a Toyota Corolla. The truck dove into the explosion crater, but was big and powerful enough to bridge over and come out the other side. Conway skidded them to a stop in the forecourt.

Chris went over the top of the cab and the other two guys jumped off the sides.

Anyone who moved received a pair of bullets in the center of their chest and another in the face.

Soon the yard was clear, but the gates had been stout enough that the building still stood intact, except for shattered windows. Gunfire began slashing down at them as BB dove through the flames and added their own guns to the fray.

16

Azadah tried to make sense of what had happened. One moment she was ladling bata rice with a spinach qorma for the guards, including the bastard who had struck her. The next moment she had once again been slammed to the ground.

She lay there wondering who had struck her this time.

No one moved toward her.

Now Mahmood lay near her on the floor as did others.

The air was thick with dust and the room looked as if a whirlwind had blown in the front doors and out the back. The electric lights were gone, but the fire still burned and lit the room, giving the dust a ruddy glow of eternal flames.

Geti had been in the kitchen doorway and now lay far across the room in a position that said she would never rise again.

And then Azadah knew.

She sat up and her head spun no more than it had since Mahmood's earlier blow.

She had not been hit.

Chris had come.

He had seen her pleadings to the sky and he had come for her. Two C. was the soldier she held at a distance with his nickname, but now the man had come for her and earned his true name in her thoughts.

As her hearing recovered, she heard the sounds of gunfire.

So did Mahmood and the other guards. Groping for their weapons, they scrambled to their feet.

No!

She was convinced in that moment Mahmood would kill Chris and she would not let that happen. She swung her ladle and caught him on the side of the face.

He yelped, then turned to face her. Surprise shifted to anger as he struck out at her. Having regained her feet, she was able to duck his first blow. Then she was aware of the iron pot still in her other hand.

Swinging it with all of her might, she slammed it into the side of head.

He staggered for a moment, dazed.

This time she spun fully around until she needed both hands to hold the pot against its desire to fly away. It smashed into the side of his head, shattering his cheek and jaw.

Still he stood.

The ladle gone, the pot snatched from her hands by the force of impact, she grabbed for the long kitchen knife on the table.

Then Mahmood twitched…and dropped to the floor like a sack of grain.

Only as he fell did she see two holes had appeared in his chest.

She spun to the face the back door.

There, on the threshold, was an apparition. A brief flash of lightning silhouetted Chris kneeling in the doorway, his rifle spitting fire.

His face lit green by the light of his night-vision goggles, Chris was shooting at the other guards in the room so quickly it might have been a single barrage, but it wasn't. In slow motion she could see each time he pulled the trigger. Could hear the bullets whistle past her. One tugged at her dress. But it wasn't a miss. Each shot was followed by the slap of bullet striking flesh behind her. Each grunt, the last gasp of a man already dead, but not yet fallen.

She turned, safe in the midst of the cloud of death, and watched the men fall until there were only the two of them in the room.

Chris rushed up to her.

He didn't take her in his arms.

He didn't kiss her madly as she had dreamed so many nights while sitting beside him under the stars.

When she looked at his eyes illuminated by the green glow of his goggles, she saw a hard man there. Yet this man she knew as well. This was Deuce, the seasoned fighter. The one she had seen him shed slowly, after each operation, over the last three months as he turned back into Chris.

"Take my belt. Hold hard. Do exactly what I do and don't let go. I have a tag-a-long," he spoke as if to someone else.

Oh. Warning the others over the radio not to shoot the person at his back.

Then he stepped by her as if he'd forgotten she was there.

17

Chris felt the reassuring tug on the back of his belt and then focused on what he had to do.

There was a dancelike flow to room-clearing. Six Delta operators hitting a target so hard, so fast, that there was no time for others to react.

The radio was no more than the occasional dance of positional calls. "B-1-3." Someone from his team—it didn't matter who—was about to enter through the third window of the first floor on the "B" side of the building—the second counting clockwise from the "A" front.

Chris called "B-1-3 inside" and the two of

them entered from opposite directions safe from each other's field of fire. In five seconds there were no unfriendlies left standing in the room.

Together they moved back along the B-wall, dropping two more guards, until they had cleared the other rooms up to "A."

"Two in five seconds, A and C," Some part of him registered a BB voice. They'd found a way to scale the building and were hitting the second floor front and back.

He and Conway surged for the front stairs. Maxwell and Jaffe were prone at opposite corners of the yard offering sniper coverage as well as targeting anyone who tried to run from the building.

18

Azadah felt as if she was being sucked along by a whirlwind.

Not once did Chris run. Instead he crouched slightly and flowed down the hall, gliding up the stairs as fast as rising smoke. By her hand wrapped hard around his belt, she could feel the perfect steadiness of his torso despite how fast his legs were moving.

In the front of the house, a raging fire shone in through the windows. Then they would plunge into an interior room and she'd be blind in the darkness except for the bright flashes from Chris' or another's weapons.

This must be how a child feels in the womb. Safe, unaware. Following in the wake of the mother/protector's every move.

It was as if she and Chris had become one. He would pause, step, turn, fire, move. She would pause, step, turn, watch another fall, move.

A room with too many to fight. They ducked back out of sight as bullets streamed forth and struck the wall opposite the doorway.

Chris slid something from his waist and tossed it into the room.

A blinding stream of light shone out, illuminating the bullet-ridden wall in stark relief, and then a shuddering bang of sound so loud that her ears ached in the hallway outside the room.

Now she knew what to do and was already rising as Chris flowed forward once more, clearing the room rapidly, each with three spits from his quiet gun.

A sudden stillness descended around them.

There was no more gunfire.

No flashes of light in the night. Now only the fire lit the rooms.

Azadah looked about. They were in a bedroom that had once been luxurious. A shattered mirror clung to a gold-painted frame big enough for two people to see themselves in. A bed of dark wood had three bodies lying upon it, their blood slowly masking the fine needlework of the spread.

Close beside her, the door of an armoire, struck with two bullets, slowly swinging open.

Out of it, the muzzle of a gun emerging.

Too late for Chris to turn.

Too late to pull him aside by the hand wrapped so firmly about his belt that she could hope it would never come free.

In her other hand…the kitchen knife.

With a swing, she sliced the blade upward in the slot.

Impact.

A cry.

The gun dropping.

And Chris' handgun firing inches from her face.

Not two shots, not three.

He emptied the entire magazine into the cabinet.

19

Chris holstered his sidearm and nudged the door open with the muzzle of his rifle.

A man slumped out of the cabinet and onto the floor.

"Syed," Azadah breathed close by his shoulder. Of course, she must have seen the files he and his men had been studying.

"A bit of overkill, Deuce," Conway observed as he joined them and looked down at the body.

At least a dozen shots had hit him.

Face, chest, neck.

There was also a nasty gash on his arm, the

single slice with which Azadah had saved his life.

"We clear?"

"Roger that."

Chris looked at his watch. He wanted to comfort Azadah. Make sure she was unhurt. He wanted to tell her things that a man only ever told one woman.

But there wasn't time.

"Five minutes. Gather intel, then we're gone."

"Roger that."

As Chris moved about the house, he was aware of the slight pressure against the small of his back. The connection through which he and Azadah had moved in such perfect harmony.

They took wallets and shot photographs. They smashed laptops and wrenched out hard drives to shove into pockets. Cell phones and USBs were gathered, but there was too much. Conway stuffed rolls of maps into a blood-stained pillowcase. Baxter and Burton slammed paper files into knapsacks.

The five minutes seemed to slide by in seconds.

Inside the front door he called over the radio, "Four—" the pressure at his waist, "Five coming out."

"Roger," Jaffe's promise that he wouldn't shoot them as they exited the building.

"Hoof it!" They raced across the forecourt, picked up the two outside men, and the seven of them dodged through the remnants of fire at the front gate. Circling the building, they sprinted across the field and headed for the open desert.

"Drone pilot, we're clear. Repeat ground team is clear. You may fire at will."

If Azadah was flagging, she didn't indicate it. She remained his shadow across the fields as if they were one united body.

There was a high shriek from above and a streak of light across the desert sky.

20

It was as bright as a lightning bolt heaved from the heavens, but straight as an arrow.

Azadah could not see the ground at her feet and could only rely on her contact with Chris to lead her to safety.

She turned her head enough to watch the lightning bolt as it struck down behind them. A ball of fire erupted back toward the heavens. Only the wall that encircled the compound kept her from being blinded.

Hellfire.

That is what the Americans had sent down on Syed's grave.

A Hellfire missile.

It was what he'd deserved.

It would hide the team's actions, for they were the silent warriors. Now it would be just another drone strike with another set of confirmed kills—confirmed by those who had already pulled the triggers before vanishing into the night.

When the rolling thunder washed over her, she looked from the fire to the men who ran near her. They had done as Chris had promised; they had returned and cut the head off the snake. Yes, it would be born anew, but it would not happen soon or well after such a blow.

Chris came to a halt and so did she. She was gasping for air, but had never felt so alive in her life.

The others gathered around and they were all watching the sky.

After the brightness of the explosion she could see nothing. Then a brief lightning flash from the dwindling storm revealed a great plane descending out of the night sky.

Chris reached back and took her hand as he turned to face her. It was stiff with being clenched so long about his belt, upon her scarf when she slept, on the last shreds of her very existence. He massaged it back to life. He slid up his night-vision gear and she could just make out his face in the light of the dying fire now a kilometer behind them across the dry grass.

"Azadah," her name was a whisper on his breath. "This plane will not land again in Afghanistan."

She felt a sudden chill. He couldn't be saying goodbye. Not here. Not after all they had been through together.

"If you step on this plane…" but he stopped.

A whisper of hope was caught in the desert wind and fluttered aloft for a moment, but faded away as he remained silent.

"Please," he started again. "Please come with me."

And born once more here in the cool air of the Afghan night, she faced him.

"I would show you my house…" Chris again fell silent.

And after being so long silent, her voice unlocked as if it had never been frozen. And the question that slid out was of her heart's making, not her mind's. "Tell me, Chris…"

And he waited for the words to fill the tiny space between them as the giant plane touched down in the desert and rolled toward them.

"Tell me that together we will make it a *home* and then I will go with you."

He brushed his hand so gently along her injured cheek that she felt no pain. "There is no greater gift you could give me," and he smiled at her.

And she knew he spoke truth, for that was the man he was.

The others were already up the ramp, but she halted one step from the clean steel slope. She thought of all the past and all the pain. Somehow it had lead to this incredible moment.

Azadah looked one last time at a night sky of emerging stars she would forever own as she stepped off a desert she would never see again.

Her home was in the heart of a man. This man. The one she would always walk beside no matter where the path lay.

For there was no greater gift than this man who had come to her from the sky.

About the Author

M. L. Buchman has over 40 novels in print. His military romantic suspense books have been named Barnes & Noble and NPR "Top 5 of the year" and *Booklist* "Top 10 of the Year." He has been nominated for the Reviewer's Choice Award for "Top 10 Romantic Suspense of 2014" by *RT Book Reviews* and the prestigous RWA RITA Award in 2016. In addition to romance, he also writes thrillers, fantasy, and science fiction.

In among his career as a corporate project manager he has: rebuilt and single-handed a fifty-foot sailboat, both flown and jumped out of airplanes, designed and built two houses, and bicycled solo around the world.

He is now making his living as a full-time writer on the Oregon Coast with his beloved wife. He is constantly amazed at what you can do with a degree in Geophysics. You may keep up with his writing and receive free extras by subscribing to his newsletter at www.mlbuchman.com.

Target Engaged (excerpt)
-a Delta Force novel-

Carla Anderson rolled up to the looming, storm-fence gate on her brother's midnight-blue Kawasaki Ninja 1000 motorcycle. The pounding of the engine against her sore butt emphasized every mile from Fort Carson in Pueblo, Colorado, home of the 4th Infantry and hopefully never again the home of

Sergeant Carla Anderson. The bike was all she had left of Clay, other than a folded flag, and she was here to honor that.

If this was the correct "here."

A small guard post stood by the gate into a broad, dusty compound. It looked deserted and she didn't see even a camera.

This *was* Fort Bragg, North Carolina. She knew that much. Two hundred and fifty square miles of military installation, not counting the addition of the neighboring Pope Army Airfield.

She'd gotten her Airborne parachute training here and had never even known what was hidden in this remote corner. Bragg was exactly the sort of place where a tiny, elite unit of the U.S. military could disappear—in plain sight.

This back corner of the home of the 82nd Airborne was harder to find than it looked. What she could see of the compound through the fence definitely ranked "worst on base."

The setup was totally whacked.

Standing outside the fence at the guard post she could see a large, squat building across the compound. The gray concrete building was incongruously cheerful with bright pink roses along the front walkway—the only landscaping visible anywhere. More recent buildings—in better condition only because they were newer—ranged off to the right. She could breach the old fence in a dozen different places just in the hundred-yard span she could see before it disappeared into a clump of scrub and low trees drooping in the June heat.

Wholly indefensible.

There was no way that this could be the headquarters of the top combat unit in any country's military.

Unless this really was their home, in which case the indefensible fence—inde-fence-ible?— was a complete sham designed to fool a sucker. She'd stick with the main gate.

She peeled off her helmet and scrubbed at her long brown hair to get some air back into her scalp. Guys always went gaga over her hair, which was a useful distraction at times. She always wore it as long as her successive commanders allowed. Pushing the limits was one of her personal life policies.

She couldn't help herself. When there was a limit, Carla always had to see just how far it could be nudged. Surprisingly far was usually the answer. Her hair had been at earlobe length in Basic. By the time she joined her first forward combat team, it brushed her jaw. Now it was down on her shoulders. It was actually something of a pain in the ass at this length—another couple inches before it could reliably ponytail—but she did like having the longest hair in the entire unit.

Carla called out a loud "Hello!" at the empty compound shimmering in the heat haze.

No response.

Using her boot in case the tall chain-link fence was electrified, she gave it a hard shake, making it rattle loudly in the dead air. Not even any birdsong in the oppressive midday heat.

A rangy man in his late forties or early fifties, his hair half gone to gray, wandered around from behind a small shack as if he just happened to be there by chance. He was dressed like any off-duty soldier: worn khaki pants, a black T-shirt, and scuffed Army boots. He slouched to a stop and tipped his head to study her from behind his Ray-Bans. He needed a haircut and a shave. This was not a soldier out to make a good first impression.

"Don't y'all get hot in that gear?" He nodded

to indicate her riding leathers without raking his eyes down her frame, which was unusual and appreciated.

"Only on warm days," she answered him. It was June in North Carolina. The temperature had crossed ninety hours ago and the air was humid enough to swim in, but complaining never got you anywhere.

"What do you need?"

So much for the pleasantries. "Looking for Delta."

"Never heard of it," the man replied with a negligent shrug. But something about how he did it told her she was in the right place.

"Combat Applications Group?" Delta Force had many names, and they certainly lived to "apply combat" to a situation. No one on the planet did it better.

His next shrug was eloquent.

Delta Lesson One: *Folks on the inside of the wire didn't call it Delta Force. It was CAG or "The Unit."* She got it. Check. Still easier to think of it as Delta though.

She pulled out her orders and held them up. "Received a set of these. Says to show up here today."

"Let me see that."

"Let me through the gate and you can look at it as long as you want."

"Sass!" He made it an accusation.

"Nope. I just don't want them getting damaged or lost maybe by accident." She offered her blandest smile with that.

"They're that important to you, girlie?"

"Yep!"

He cracked what might have been the start of a grin, but it didn't get far on that grim face. Then he opened the gate and she idled the bike forward, scuffing her boots through the dust.

From this side she could see that the chain link was wholly intact. There was a five-meter swath of scorched earth inside the fence line. Through the heat haze, she could see both infrared and laser spy eyes down the length of the wire. And that was only the defenses she could see. So…a very *not* inde-fence-ible fence. Absolutely the right place.

When she went to hold out the orders, he waved them aside.

"Don't you want to see them?" This had to be the right place. She was the first woman in history to walk through The Unit's gates by order. A part of her wanted the man to acknowledge that. Any man. A Marine Corps marching band wouldn't have been out of order.

She wanted to stand again as she had on that very first day, raising her right hand. "I, Carla Anderson, do solemnly swear that I will support and defend the Constitution…"

She shoved that aside. The only man's acknowledgment she'd ever cared about was her big brother's, and he was gone.

The man just turned away and spoke to her over his shoulder as he closed the gate behind her bike. "Go ahead and check in. You're one of the last to arrive. We start in a couple hours"—as if it were a blasted dinner party. "And I already saw those orders when I signed them. Now put them away before someone else sees them and thinks you're still a soldier." He walked away.

She watched the man's retreating back. *He'd* signed her orders?

That was the notoriously hard-ass Colonel Charlie Brighton?

What the hell was the leader of the U.S. Army's Tier One asset doing manning the gate? Duh…assessing new applicants.

This place *was* whacked. Totally!

There were only three Tier One assets in the entire U.S. military. There was Navy's Special Warfare Development Group, DEVGRU, that the public thought was called SEAL Team Six—although it hadn't been named that for thirty years now. There was the Air Force's 24th STS—which pretty much no one on the outside had ever heard of. And there was the 1st Special Forces Operational Detachment—Delta—whose very existence was still denied by the Pentagon despite four decades of operations, several books, and a couple of seriously off-the-mark movies that were still fun to watch because Chuck Norris kicked ass even under the stupidest of circumstances.

Total Tier One women across all three teams? Zero.

About to be? One. Staff Sergeant First Class Carla Anderson.

Where did she need to go to check in? There was no signage. No drill sergeant hovering. No—

Delta Lesson Number Two: *You aren't in the Army anymore, sister.*

No longer a soldier, as the Colonel had

said, at least not while on The Unit's side of the fence. On this side they weren't regular Army; they were "other."

If that meant she had to take care of herself, well, that was a lesson she'd learned long ago. Against stereotype, her well-bred, East Coast white-guy dad was the drunk. Her dirt-poor half Tennessee Cherokee, half Colorado settler mom, who'd passed her dusky skin and dark hair on to her daughter, had been a sober and serious woman. She'd also been a casualty of an Afghanistan dust-bowl IED while serving in the National Guard. Carla's big brother Clay now lay beside Mom in Arlington National Cemetery. Dead from a training accident. Except your average training accident didn't include a posthumous rank bump, a medal, and coming home in a sealed box reportedly with no face.

Clay had flown helicopters in the Army's 160th SOAR with the famous Majors Beale and Henderson. Well, famous in the world of people who'd flown with the Special Operations Aviation Regiment, or their little sisters who'd begged for stories of them whenever big brothers were home on leave. Otherwise totally invisible.

Clay had clearly died on a black op that she'd never be told a word of, so she didn't bother asking. Which was okay. He knew the risks, just as Mom had. Just as she herself had when she'd signed up the day of Clay's funeral, four years ago. She'd been on the front lines ever since and so far lived to tell about it.

Carla popped Clay's Ninja—which is how she still thought of it, even after riding it for four years—back into first and rolled it slowly up to the building with the pink roses. As good a place to start as any.

***

"Hey, check out this shit!"

Sergeant First Class Kyle Reeves looked out the window of the mess hall at the guy's call. Sergeant Ralph last-name-already-forgotten was 75th Rangers and too damn proud of it.

Though…damn! Ralphie was onto something.

Kyle would definitely check out *this shit*.

Babe on a hot bike, looking like she knew how to handle it.

Through the window, he inspected her lean length as she clambered off the machine.

Army boots. So call her five-eight, a hundred
and thirty, and every part that wasn't amazing
curves looked like serious muscle. Hair
the color of lush, dark caramel brushed her
shoulders but moved like the finest silk, her
skin permanently the color of the darkest tan.
Women in magazines didn't look that hot.
Those women always looked anorexic to him
anyway, even the pinup babes displayed on
Hesco barriers at forward operating bases up
in the Hindu Kush where he'd done too much
of the last couple years.

This woman didn't look like that for a
second. She looked powerful. And dangerous.

Her tight leathers revealed muscles made
of pure soldier.

Ralph Something moseyed out of the mess-
hall building where the hundred selectees
were hanging out to await the start of the next
testing class at sundown.

Well, Kyle sure wasn't going to pass up the
opportunity for a closer look. Though seeing
Ralph's attitude, Kyle hung back a bit so that
he wouldn't be too closely associated with the
dickhead.

Ralph had been spoiling for a fight ever

since he'd found out he was one of the least experienced guys to show up for Delta selection. He was from the 75th Ranger Regiment, but his deployments hadn't seen much action. Each of his attempts to brag for status had gotten him absolutely nowhere.

Most of the guys here were 75th Rangers, 82nd Airborne, or Green Beret Special Forces like himself. And most had seen a shitload of action because that was the nature of the world at the moment. There were a couple SEALs who hadn't made SEAL Team Six and probably weren't going to make Delta, a dude from the Secret Service Hostage Rescue Team who wasn't going to last a day no matter how good a shot he was, and two guys who were regular Army.

The question of the moment though, who was she?

Her biking leathers were high-end, sewn in a jagged lightning-bolt pattern of yellow on smoke gray. It made her look like she was racing at full tilt while standing still. He imagined her hunched over her midnight-blue machine and hustling down the road at her Ninja's top speed—which was north of 150.

He definitely had to see that one day.

Kyle blessed the inspiration on his last leave that had made him walk past the small Toyota pickup that had looked so practical and buy the wildfire-red Ducati Multistrada 1200 instead. Pity his bike was parked around the back of the barracks at the moment. Maybe they could do a little bonding over their rides. Her machine looked absolutely cherry.

Much like its rider.

Ralph walked right up to her with all his arrogant and stupid hanging out for everyone to see. The other soldiers began filtering outside to watch the show.

"Well, girlie, looks like you pulled into the wrong spot. This here is Delta territory."

Kyle thought about stopping Ralph, thought that someone should give the guy a good beating, but Dad had taught him control. He would take Ralph down if he got aggressive, but he really didn't want to be associated with the jerk, even by grabbing him back.

The woman turned to face them, then unzipped the front of her jacket in one of those long, slow movie moves. The sunlight shimmered across her hair as she gave it an "unthinking" toss. Wraparound dark glasses hid her eyes, adding to the mystery.

He could see what there was of Ralph's brain imploding from lack of blood. He felt the effect himself despite standing a half-dozen paces farther back.

She wasn't hot; she sizzled. Her parting leathers revealed an Army green T-shirt and proof that the very nice contours suggested by her outer gear were completely genuine. Her curves weren't big—she had a lean build—but they were as pure woman as her shoulders and legs were pure soldier.

"There's a man who called me 'girlie' earlier." Her voice was smooth and seductive, not low and throaty, but rich and filled with nuance.

She sounded like one of those people who could hypnotize a Cobra, either the snake or the attack helicopter.

"He's a bird colonel. He can call me that if he wants. You aren't nothing but meat walking on sacred ground and wishing he belonged."

Kyle nodded to himself. The "girlie" got it in one.

"*You*"—she jabbed a finger into Sergeant

Ralph Something's chest—"do not get 'girlie' privileges. *We* clear?"

"Oh, sweetheart, I can think of plenty of privileges that you'll want to be giving to—" His hand only made it halfway to stroking her hair.

If Kyle hadn't been Green Beret trained, he wouldn't have seen it because she moved so fast and clean.

"—*me!*" Ralph's voice shot upward on a sharp squeak.

The woman had Ralph's pinkie bent to the edge of dislocation and, before the man could react, had leveraged it behind his back and upward until old Ralph Something was perched on his toes trying to ease the pressure. With her free hand, she shoved against the middle of his back to send him stumbling out of control into the concrete wall of the mess hall with a loud *clonk* when his head hit.

Minimum force, maximum result. The Unit's way.

She eased off on his finger and old Ralph dropped to the dirt like a sack of potatoes. He didn't move much.

"Oops." She turned to face the crowd that had gathered.

She didn't even have to say, "Anyone else?" Her look said plenty.

Kyle began to applaud. He wasn't the only one, but he was in the minority. Most of the guys were doing a wait and see.

A couple looked pissed.

Everyone knew that the Marines' combat training had graduated a few women, but that was just jarheads on the ground.

This was Delta. The Unit was Tier One. A Special Mission Unit. They were supposed to be the one true bastion of male dominance. No one had warned them that a woman was coming in.

Just one woman, Kyle thought. The first one. How exceptional did that make her? Pretty damn was his guess. Even if she didn't last the first day, still pretty damn. And damn pretty. He'd bet on dark eyes behind her wraparound shades. She didn't take them off, so it was a bet he'd have to settle later on.

A couple corpsmen came over and carted Ralph Something away even though he was already sitting up—just dazed with a bloody cut on his forehead.

The Deltas who'd come out to watch the

show from a few buildings down didn't say a word before going back to whatever they'd been doing.

Kyle made a bet with himself that Ralph Something wouldn't be showing up at sundown's first roll call. They'd just lost the first one of the class and the selection process hadn't even begun. Or maybe it just had.

"Where's check-in?" Her voice really was as lush as her hair, and it took Kyle a moment to focus on the actual words.

He pointed at the next building over and received a nod of thanks.

That made watching her walk away in those tight leathers strictly a bonus.

Available at fine retailers everywhere.

Other works by M.L. Buchman

Newsletter signup at:
www.mlbuchman.com

Printed in Great Britain
by Amazon